The Easter Beagle Returns!

Based on the comic strip and
characters created by Charles M. Schulz
Adapted by Alice Alfonsi
Art adapted by Peter and Nick LoBianco

LITTLE SIMON

New York   London   Toronto   Sydney

LITTLE SIMON
An imprint of Simon & Schuster Children's Publishing Division
1230 Avenue of the Americas, New York, New York 10020
Copyright © 2004 by United Feature Syndicate, Inc. All rights reserved.
PEANUTS is a registered trademark of United Feature Syndicate, Inc.
All rights reserved, including the right of reproduction in whole or in part in any form.
LITTLE SIMON and colophon are registered trademarks of Simon & Schuster.
Manufactured in the United States of America
First Edition 10 9 8 7 6 5 4 3 2 1
ISBN 0-689-86588-0
Based on the comic strips by Charles M. Schulz

Easter morning was almost here! Everyone was excited about the return of the world-famous Easter Beagle. Everyone but Charlie Brown.

Lucy showed Charlie Brown her empty Easter basket. It had taken her weeks to decorate it.

"So you *finally* made up your mind," Charlie Brown said. "Incredible."

"I may have taken a long time to decide, but I had to be sure. This isn't just any old Easter basket," Lucy said as she marched off in a huff.

Charlie Brown didn't understand the fuss over Easter or the Easter Beagle. To get his mind off the whole thing Charlie Brown went to visit his friend Linus.

"I've been thinking about a holiday time-saver," Linus told Charlie Brown. "Why couldn't I send the same form letter to the Great Pumpkin, Santa Claus, and the Easter Beagle? Those guys get so much mail that I bet they don't even read the letters themselves!"

"You can't do that!" cried Charlie Brown.

"Why not?" said Linus. "The trouble with you, Charlie Brown, is you don't understand how these big organizations work."

"What about you, Charlie Brown?" Linus asked. "You should write a letter to the Easter Beagle. Don't you want the Easter Beagle to bring you something special for Easter?"

"A letter won't make a difference," said Charlie Brown. "The Easter Beagle never brings me anything anyway."

"You just don't have the Easter spirit," Linus said.

Charlie Brown sighed and headed for the door. So much for getting his mind off the Easter Beagle!

Across town Peppermint Patty was a nervous wreck. Last Easter, Marcie had fried the Easter eggs, baked the Easter eggs, and waffled the Easter eggs. She had even made Easter egg soup!

Peppermint Patty ran to the backyard. She found Marcie standing by a table.

"Eggs boiled as ordered, Sir!" Marcie said. Peppermint Patty stared at the perfectly prepared eggs. Easter Beagle or no Easter Beagle, this holiday was looking better already.

Later that day Charlie Brown and his friends played their annual Easter baseball game. As usual, Peppermint Patty's team was winning and Charlie Brown's team was losing.

On home plate Peppermint Patty held the bat and waited for the pitch.

"Throw it past 'er, pitcher!" Lucy cried from the outfield. Charlie Brown threw the ball as hard as he could.

POW!
A hit! The ball whizzed past Charlie Brown so fast
it blew him off the pitcher's mound. His baseball glove,
shoes, socks, shirt, and baseball cap went flying!

As Peppermint Patty circled the bases for the winning run, Lucy walked up to Charlie Brown and smiled. "Oooo! You look so cute lying there with your little Easter toes sparkling in the sun," she told him.

"*ARRRGGGHHH!* Get back in center field where you belong!" Charlie Brown shouted.

"How can a pitcher be so crabby at Easter time?" Lucy wondered aloud.
"You need a visit from the Easter Beagle."

"The Easter Beagle! The Easter Beagle!" Charlie Brown cried. "I am
tired of hearing about the Easter Beagle!"

Then, with the game lost, Charlie Brown picked up his clothes and
headed home.

The next morning was Easter! Linus woke up early to greet the Easter Beagle. One hour went by. Then two. Then three. But there was no sign of the Easter Beagle.

"Where could he be?" Linus cried.

Linus went out to look for the Easter Beagle. He didn't have to go far. Snoopy was still sleeping on his doghouse.

"You're not up yet!" Linus said. "Kids all over the world are waiting for the Easter Beagle. You can't disappoint them!"

Snoopy rolled over and covered his ears. He had stayed up late eating pizza, drinking root beer, and reading letters to the Easter Beagle. Now he was too tired to deliver Easter eggs.

"You've got to get out there and deliver those eggs!" Linus told Snoopy. "It's your job! It's your duty!"

Snoopy sat up and yawned. He was about to close his eyes again when Linus pushed an Easter basket full of eggs into Snoopy's paws.

"Now get out there!" Linus cried.

Feeling dizzy, Snoopy trudged off to deliver the Easter eggs. But he didn't feel like the Easter Beagle at all. Snoopy was so tired he didn't dance his Easter dance or smile his Easter smile.

Sally and Lucy watched the Easter Beagle pass them by without even tossing an egg.

"What do you think of that?" Sally said. "It's Scrooge at Easter."

Snoopy didn't want to deliver Easter eggs. Couldn't the Easter Beagle skip a year?

He was just about to turn around and go back to his doghouse when he ran into Woodstock. His little friend chirped happily. He had his own Easter basket under his wing. That gave Snoopy an idea. The Easter Beagle would indeed return this year!

A few minutes later Linus looked out his window. A giant colored egg now sat in his front yard.

"Wow!" Linus cried.

Sally came running to see what her Sweet Babboo was excited about. "What is it?" Sally asked. Then she saw the giant egg. Sally was amazed too. "That's the biggest egg I've ever seen," said Linus. "The Easter Beagle has done it again!"

Suddenly the Easter egg burst open with a loud *CRACK!* Out came the Easter Beagle, riding on a unicycle and juggling Easter eggs while Woodstock perched on his head.

"You have to give the Easter Beagle credit," Linus told Sally. "Each year he comes up with a better entrance!"

"Thanks!" said Franklin as Snoopy tossed him an Easter egg.

"Thank you very much," Schroeder said when Snoopy gave him an egg.

"Thank you! Thank you!" cried Marcie and Peppermint Patty.

When Snoopy met Lucy he gave her an Easter egg. He also gave her a great big Easter kiss on the cheek.

"Yuck! Dog germs!" Lucy cried.

"What about me?" Sally cried.
Snoopy's Easter basket was empty. So he gave Sally
the only thing he had left—an Easter basket bonnet.